The Rise Of The Three-Eyed King

Leah Z. Declaro

Ukiyoto Publishing

All global publishing rights are held by

Ukiyoto Publishing

Published in 2023

Content Copyright © Leah Z. Declaro
ISBN 9789360163532

All rights reserved.

No part of this publication may be reproduced, transmitted, or stored in a retrieval system, in any form by any means, electronic, mechanical, photocopying, recording or otherwise, without the prior permission of the publisher.

The moral rights of the author have been asserted.

This is a work of fiction. Names, characters, businesses, places, events, locales, and incidents are either the products of the author's imagination or used in a fictitious manner. Any resemblance to actual persons, living or dead, or actual events is purely coincidental.

This book is sold subject to the condition that it shall not by way of trade or otherwise, be lent, resold, hired out or otherwise circulated, without the publisher's prior consent, in any form of binding or cover other than that in which it is published.

www.ukiyoto.com

Dedication

I dedicate this book to my late mother, Romelia M. Zarriz. She is my inspiration in writing and I know she is the first person who is happy for me because one of my dreams of having my book came true. Wherever she is now, I will thank her with all my heart and remember her for the rest of my life.

I also dedicate this work to my very supportive husband and my two children.

Most of all to God for giving me the talent to create a good story.

Contents

Chapter 1	1
Chapter 2	3
Chapter 3	5
Chapter 4	8
Chapter 5	10
Chapter 6	13
Chapter 7	18
Chapter 8	26
About the Author	29

Chapter 1

In the palace of Tonga, the love of the king and queen evolved. They have been together for seven years but they have not yet been blessed with a child. King Gerom was very upset because he wants a child to inherit his kingdom when the time come.

He summons sorcerers from all corners of the kingdom to impregnate the queen. Almost all those he summoned failed to impregnate his wife. The king hardly knew what to do. Sometimes he thought that one of them might have a disparity.

"I don't want this to happen to us, Queen Ferolina. You need to get pregnant by the second appearance of the full moon," King Gerom sadly notified the queen.

"But how, my beloved king? I am worried about the situation between the two of us. I followed all the counselors' advice just to get pregnant. What are we going to do?" Queen Ferolina almost cried too. You can see the disappointment in her beautiful eyes.

Until one day, an old man with a long beard got lost in the palace. The guards immediately kicked him out because his appearance was so filthy. His clothes were torn, his feet were muddy too, and his grey and wavy hair looked like years hadn't combed it.

"You don't belong in this place. Go away and the king might see you and kill you or feed you to the hungry crocodiles in the creek!" a soldier snorted at him.

Instead of being startled, the old man laughed foolishly.

"The king is soft-hearted. He will not hurt me but I am what the king needs to get the queen pregnant. I am what the king needs. He needs me!"

When the soldier heard what the old man said, he immediately approached him and then asked him calmly.

"What did you say? How did you know the king needed help to get the queen pregnant? Who are you?" The soldier became interested because they knew how much the king wanted his queen to get pregnant.

"I know how the queen to be pregnant but I won't tell it. I know something about how to get the queen pregnant but I won't tell it. La la la la..." The old man said repeatedly and continued to sing and was about to leave but the soldier stopped him and grabbed his arm.

"You cannot leave. You will tell what you know, or I will inform the king and you will be punished!"

"Aren't you letting me go? So I am leaving. But let me tell you, I know a lot and I am the only one who will be the key to the king and the queen having a child." The old man continued to crack up and was about to leave the palace again.

The soldier was about to stop the old man when in an instant, he disappeared and could not be caught. The soldier just returned to his post and regretted what the old man could do for the king and queen to have a child.

The soldier did not spurn what happened. He immediately asked permission to speak to the king.

The king immediately let him into his vast library. There, the soldier told what he found out about the old man who could know how to get the queen pregnant.

When the king heard that, he immediately called all the soldiers to search the entire forest.

"You have to bring me what Noem used to say. If that stranger old man is the answer to what we have been asking for a long time, I am ready to give half of my wealth," King Gerom informed confidently.

The soldiers immediately adhered to the king's order. They searched the entire forest area of the kingdom. Darkness reached them in the forest, but neither the shadow of the old man nor a small dwelling where he could live, they saw nothing.

Chapter 2

The soldiers sadly informed King Gerom that they had not seen the old man. The king's shoulders also fell and he tried to control his anger.

For several nights the king could not sleep. The old man that Noem said could not evade in his mind. The queen was also worried because of the depth of the king's thoughts.

"My king, rest your mind first. In the next few days, we must prepare. Have you forgotten that King Herod's camp will attack the palace?"

"I know. I was just too disturbed by what Noem said. I want us to have an heir very soon. The time of judgment is near but no one will replace my kingdom yet. I can't agree, we need to see that old man as soon as possible," said the king worriedly.

"Why don't we just go to Mother Magda, and see if she can help us? Let's forget the past," said the queen gently.

"No. She has nothing to do with us. Let us sleep now. Tomorrow, I will call a meeting for the rest of the palace's compatriots to further strengthen our soldiers. I know that King Herod's camp will not succeed."

Almost everything was ready for the invasion of the camp of King Herod's kingdom in the palace. Everyone has their place so that the opponents cannot succeed. King Gerom made sure that the weapons were complete and stable so that they could win the battle.

Due to the preparation for the enemy's invasion, King Gerom temporarily forgot about the old man.

Until the day of the invasion came. The king's momentary rest was shattered when the soldier smashed his extensive library.

"King Gerom, the soldiers of the other kingdom are coming. They are numerous and the arrows are already flying. Most of our other soldiers are also wounded. They are twice as many as us!" a soldier shouted, shocking the king.

"What? I thought everything was ready. Do not let the enemies enter the palace. Prepare spears with fire on the tip. They must be hit so they all die!" King Gerom immediately ordered.

The battle lasted three hours. All the prepared weapons of the palace were used to destroy the enemies, many enemies also died but King Gerom's soldiers died more.

Queen Ferolina cried and cried. The king did not let her out. She was only inside their vast room but she could watch what was happening by peeking at the top of the tower.

She was accompanied by her five assistants. They are all fearful about what was happening and the queen wants to go out to see her beloved king.

"Do not go out, dear queen, it is too dangerous when you go out. Flying arrows may hit us. Let's get here and wait for the signal of King Gerom," Veronica stopped her.

"But, Veronica. I am too worried. I am so afraid. Maybe King Herod will seize the palace from us. How are we? How is the kingdom? How is my beloved king?" The queen's shoulders were shaking.

Her heart was full of fear because of what happened.

"Do not be afraid, Queen Ferolina. We will know that King Herod will not win. We will put our full trust in our beloved king and the remaining brave soldiers. We will not lose hope. This battle will end with victory for us," Sarina comforting the queen.

Unfortunately, King Herod's camp had almost taken over the entire palace. The rest of King Gerom's soldiers are wounded.

"Give up, King Gerom. There is nothing you can do, your palace will be mine!" King Herod shouted. He knew they were going to win the fight.

"I will not give up. I will never give you my kingdom. You are so shameless. You are greedy!" King Gerom also loudly shouted.

He hides behind a wide mirror. The two other soldiers who were left to protect him were also behind him.

Chapter 3

King Gerom did nothing. Only ten of his soldiers were left alive. King Herod's soldiers also tied them up. Some of the horses in the palace had also perished from the wounds caused by the burning arrows.

The forces of the enemies were more powerful so King Gerom's camp was defeated. This is a very tragic incident that happened in the kingdom. The king was almost in tears as he watched the blood flow throughout the palace. He also felt sorry for his soldiers because of the failed fight.

"You are out of power, King Gerom. Come out of your hiding place. You are surrounded by my soldiers. Your kingdom is mine whether you want it or not!" King Herod shouted laughingly. He was still sitting in the middle of the palace as if he was already the new king of the kingdom.

Unfortunately, King Herod's soldiers also captured King Gerom. Queen Ferolina was also captured along with her servants. Their hearts were almost downtrodden by the nightmare.

King Herod kicked them out of the palace. They did nothing but ride the horse out of the palace. King Gerom and Queen Ferolina did not have a single thing with them. The rest of their soldiers were left in the palace to serve. Against their will, they did nothing because they lost the bloody battle.

The king and queen have travelled a long way. Whitey, their horse, was almost out of breath from the distance of their journey. They felt hungry and tired. Darkness overtook them until they reached the middle of the forest exceptionally far away from the palace.

After some time, King Gerom and Queen Ferolina lived a normal life in the middle of the forest. Through the pieces of wood around, King Gerom made a small hut, just enough for the two of them.

Their lifestyle used to be luxurious and it was very different from where they were in the forest. They feel cold and chill especially when it rains heavily.

Later, they also learned to live in the forest, they only eat fruits that can be found around. There is a stream at the end of the forest where they drink and bathe. They used patches of wood leaves to cover their bodies. It seems that their new home has become a paradise for them.

One day while King Gerom was gathering food, he heard a faint cry.

"Help, help me! Have mercy, help me!"

He immediately went to the source of the voice. He was shocked when he saw a big snake coiling around the body of the old man. He could barely breathe.

"Beloved King, help me!"

King Gerom was surprised again because the old man knew him.

He moved toward him but he could not remember who the old man was coiling up by the snake.

"Have mercy, help me..." lamented the old man again.

The king panicked and immediately looked for something he could beat the big snake with. He also thought that it could not be killed because it was almost the size of a tree that had been standing in the forest for a long time.

His attention was drawn to the sword stuck in the big rock. He had never seen it in the middle of the forest before.

He was amazed because it was so lustrous and the handle seemed to be made of silver and designed with a dragon. He immediately touched it and tried to pull it out but it seemed to be buried in the rock. He used all his strength to draw the sword but it still can't be pulled out.

"Shout the *'Three-eyed'*, beloved king. Hurry up, the snake is about to devour me!" the old man informed him.

Although surprised, King Gerom followed what the old man ordered.

"Three-eyed!" he shouted and his eyes widened as he drew the sword.

It shines in the sunlight. Its tip is sharp and shiny. King Gerom's hands trembled as he gripped the sword tightly. In all his life as a king, he had only now held such a beautiful sword. It seems strange and magical.

He saw that the mouth of the snake had opened and it was ready to swallow the old man whole. King Gerom did not know what strength he had as he held the sword.

"My King, hurry up..." The old man's voice was very flimsy.

Some kind of force shrouded the king's body and he immediately thrust the sharp sword into the snake. It was hit right in the throat. It seemed like an earthquake and tornado passed through the middle of the forest when the snake's body flipped.

In an instant, the huge snake suddenly disappeared. The king looked around but did not see the big snake anymore. He rubbed his eyes and seemed to be dreaming.

"Thank you very much, beloved King Gerom. You saved my life. I owe you why I got rid of Poseude," the old man calmly said while still holding his neck, which was also swathed by the snake.

There the king remembered the old man he had helped. He immediately stood up and held him by the arm.

"Why do you know me? Who are you? Why do you know how to pull this sword out of the big stone? Where did it come from? Who is Poseude?" the king asked one after another.

"You will know everything, at the right time," replied the old man.

It seems like a puzzle to the king.

Chapter 4

King Gerom took the old man to their small hut. Even Queen Ferolina was surprised to see the old man.

"Who is he, my King? What happened to him and he seems to have scars on his body?"

King Gerom told the story of what happened to the queen. The queen sparked her eyes when she heard the king's story, especially about the sword.

"Where is the sword? Why didn't you bring it home?" she asked the king.

"After the big snake disappeared from the surroundings, the sword also returned to the big stone on its own. I blinked for a moment, and it suddenly disappeared into the middle of the forest. I don't know what mystery prevailed earlier. It seems that the old man with me knows something," explained the king.

"May I know your name? Where do you come from? What do you know about the king's story? How did you know he was the king of Tonga then? What does that snake have to do with the sword?" Queen Ferolina asked the old man full of curiosity.

Since the old man's body was still weak, he quickly lay down on the floor. The queen also quickly took hot water and then wiped his forehead and treated the scars on his body with the extracts of medicinal plants growing in the surroundings. They also felt sorry for the old man because his strength seemed to have been exhausted by the snake coiling around his entire body.

The king also looked for fruits for them to eat. What happened is still a mystery to him. He couldn't believe especially the strength he possessed when he held the magical sword.

"Thank you very much, beloved King and Queen, for taking care of me. May your union be fruitful and you will regain the kingdom of

Tonga from the hands of the oppressive king, King Herod," said the old man that night. His strength returned especially when he drank the hot juice of stewed star leaves.

The king and queen looked at each other because the old man seemed to know something about their kingdom.

In the middle of the night, the king and queen fell asleep. The old man was also lying on a small pallet. He got up and saw the sleeping king and queen on the other side. Suddenly his eyes flashed. Something came out of his mouth that only he could hear. In an instant, he suddenly disappeared like smoke in the void.

The next morning, Queen Ferolina immediately looked for the old man to drink the hot extract of the star leaf but she did not see him. King Gerom also looked for the old man all around but there was not even a shadow of the old man. He returned to the forest where the snake coiled around the old man and even the big rock where the sword was gone. There were many questions in the king's mind, but he had no clear answer.

Meanwhile, in the kingdom of Tonga, the poor merchants were all crying and complaining about King Herod's new rule. A sixty percent tax was taken from businessmen. Failure to pay correctly was punished by soldiers on the king's orders.

"No one will complain about my rules. I am the new king and no one will disobey. Remember that I own the kingdom and if you don't want to obey, you already know the answer. My soldiers will whip your body and I will take all your earnings. Be thankful because I still allow you to sell in my territory. Is that clear?" said the king proudly as he toured the entire establishment.

The merchants had no choice but to bow down and agree to the king's order even against their will.

King Herod became powerful and even richer. His name became known throughout Asia. Everyone is afraid of him. He is also looking for King Gerom and Queen Ferolina to make them helpers in his kingdom but no one can tell where they are.

Chapter 5

A month later, the old man did not appear in the forest. What Noem had said about the old man who had entered the palace came back to King Gerom's memory. He was suddenly agitated and wanted to see him again and maybe the old man who entered the palace before and whom he helped was the same one.

"Beloved king. Look, my stomach seems to have grown. I feel strange. I can't explain it but it feels like something inside," the queen happily informed while the king was outside their hut.

"What do you mean, my queen?" the king also asked eagerly.

"It's like I'm pregnant. My period hasn't come. There's something strange inside my stomach. I want to eat a dragon's egg. If you can, find me as soon as possible."

The king's eyes widened upon hearing what the Queen's said. Suddenly, his surroundings light up and he can't explain the happiness he feels. His dream will come true, they will have an heir. However, he suddenly felt sad because he would not be able to inherit anything from their future child. The kingdom is gone and they are poor now.

"Aren't you happy if I'm pregnant? Haven't we been dreaming about this for a long time? Why are you suddenly sad? Don't you want it?" The queen noticed the king's sadness.

"I am happy, my queen. I was only sad for a moment because the kingdom is gone. We will not bequeath anything to our future son. I am sorry because I was not able to protect the palace, our people, our properties, our kingdom, and all our dreams," answered King Gerom sadly.

"Don't think about that, beloved king. The important thing is that we are together. I don't need the wealth or the kingdom because I am with you. This place is our new kingdom, it's more peaceful, away from trouble and we don't starve. It is a paradise for us." The queen also eases the king's feelings.

A few more months passed, and Queen Ferolina's stomach became more and more outsized. Her feelings are different every day since conception. No matter how hard it was, King Gerom persevered in pursuing the queen's desires. Even the dragon's egg was obtained by him from the distant mountain of Waxian. Nothing was impossible for him and even he did not know why he had such strength to win what he wanted for the queen.

Until one day, the queen complained of stomach pain. It was about to explode so she screamed. King Gerom was also confused because he didn't know what to do.

Suddenly, an old woman entered their small hut. It seems that she knows that Queen Ferolina is about to give birth.

"Don't lose hope, Queen Ferolina. I will take care of you. You'll bring your child out healthy," she said, surprising the king and queen.

Queen Ferolina allotted her full force for a few minutes before a healthy baby was released. King Gerom could barely breathe while walking back and forth. Even though there was a question in his mind as to how the old woman suddenly appeared to help the queen in giving birth, still he was thankful.

"King Gerom. The baby has been delivered. A very healthy baby boy. He will be the next king of Tonga," the old woman said meaningfully.

The king immediately entered the hut. His happiness was mixed when the old woman handed him the baby wrapped in deer skin. The heat that flowed through the king's blood was strange when his son's skin touched next to him. But he was greatly shocked because the baby did not only have two eyes. It still has an eye on its forehead.

"What happened? Why is our son like this? Why does he have three eyes? Is he human?" The king's voice grew louder but the old woman suddenly disappeared.

Queen Ferolina temporarily lost consciousness due to the strong force during her delivery.

Even though it hurt the king's feelings, he tried to accept the condition of their son.

A few years passed, and Hongwe quickly grew up to be strong, kind, and enthusiastic about everything.

King Gerom also trained his son in fighting at the age of eight. By the time he reached the age of twelve, Hongwe had become an expert in any field of forest animal fighting.

He also knows how to do karate with his father's patience. Queen Ferolina also made her feel a strong love for her son even though she questioned his strange appearance.

Life in the kingdom of Tonga became more thorny due to the cruel rule of King Herod. King Herod's son, Prince Tzungwo, grew up at the same time as Hongwe. They are almost the same age. He was also cruel to the soldiers and poor people in the kingdom as his father the king taught him.

Prince Tzungwo almost beat the merchants who could not pay the sixty percent tax because their income was not enough. He has no mercy and no care. He will also inherit the kingdom of Tonga when the time comes. King Herod was very happy with the authority and discernment of his son.

"You will be a brave and well-known king in the future. I am proud of you and I am happy because you are my heir, Prince Tzungwo," said King Herod to his son, while he was being massaged by the beautiful masseuses.

All the beautiful women that Tzungwo likes will be convened to the palace and he plays with and abuses their virginity.

Even against their will, they can't do anything because they don't have the power to suppress the evil of King Herod and Tzungwo. Even the queen can't do anything because she is also controlled by the king.

Only the lady Zobel was the only one he didn't see because her parents were hiding her. They know how evil and animalistic Tzungwo's behavior just like his father king. Zobel grew up to be very beautiful, kind, and charming. But she does not leave the house as a woman. Her mother made her dress in men's clothes so that Tzungwo wouldn't recognize her.

Chapter 6

Six years passed, and Hongwe became a full-fledged young man. Even though he has three eyes, his natural masculinity can still be seen. Any woman will be fascinated by the posture and solidity of his body. He is also adept at heavy labor. Even wild animals in the forest can be tamed by him. Animals and birds also became tame to him.

One day, Hongwe asked his father for permission to leave the forest. He wants to see the former kingdom ruled by his father but Queen Ferolina did not agree when she heard it.

"I don't want you to go to that place, Hongwe. It is very dangerous and King Herod might find out that you are our son and what will be done against you. I can't bear that," pleaded the queen.

"Do not worry, my mother queen. They won't recognize me. I will also hide my appearance. I just want to know what the situation of the kingdom is. The time will come that the kingdom will be returned to us," answered Hongwe bravely to his mother.

Even against the will of the queen, she did nothing. King Gerom also allowed his son and gave his blessing to go to the kingdom of Tonga. He has trust in his son and knows his strength.

Hongwe also grew up smart, he knew what he was doing. Riding the horse Whitey, Hongwe reached the kingdom. He was still far away and he could see the brutality the soldiers were doing to the merchants. They also whip the naked workers who move slowly while loading some materials to build a large temple.

Hongwe tied Whitey to a tree near the creek. He was wearing a thick deerskin. He needed something new to wear so he could pretend to be a palace soldier. It seems that chance also agreed with him because in the distance a soldier was sleeping on the grass. Perhaps he rested for a while away from the temple under construction. Hongwe immediately covered the mouth of the soldier so as not to make any noise. Due to the force of his punch in the soldier's stomach, he immediately lost consciousness.

Hongwe wasted no time. He took off the soldier's clothes he was wearing and immediately put them on. It fits him well even though the soldier is big. So that the soldier wouldn't wake up, he hit his head with a big stone and he completely lost his life. Since Hongwe was not used to many people, he was outnumbered when he reached the palace grounds. He also secured his forehead to be covered so that his third eye could not be seen.

There, Hongwe witnessed how cruel the palace soldiers were to the workers. In the crowd, he was hardly noticed from where he was standing. Suddenly, everyone knelt when the flock of soldiers came in a chariot. They almost worshiped when the two strong men came out. One was wearing a crown, and Hongwe realized he was the king of Tonga.

Since Hongwe did not know what people do when the king comes, he did not bow to pay respect to the king and his son. Prince Tzungwo immediately caught him and grabbed him from the soldiers.

"Who are you not to show respect to those in authority and power? You may have forgotten that we are the ones who devour you! Come on, bend down and kiss my feet!" Tzungwo ordered Hongwe loudly.

Hongwe's ears heated and he wanted to grab the man in front of him. He thought that his plan might be ruined if he showed his true personality and he certainly did not have enough power for the number of soldiers surrounding him.

Against his will, he kissed Tzungwo's feet and was shocked when a whip hit his body.

"That is good enough with a reprimanded soldier like you! The next time I see you just standing there and doing nothing, I will let you crawl on the ground like a snake!" Tzungwo's eyes widened with anger.

Hongwe also endured the whipping that hit his body.

All the soldiers laughed as Tzungwo beat Hongwe's whole body with a whip. Zobel couldn't believe it when she witnessed it. What she knows is that all the soldiers in the kingdom are cruel but the soldier that Tzungwo is beating seems strange to her and he doesn't seem to know the policy of the palace.

When the king and his companions left, Zobel immediately approached Hongwe who was writhing in pain. She knew his body was full of bruises.

"Come, I will help you up. I will treat your wounds." Zobel didn't know why she felt so comfortable with the stranger even though he was a palace soldier.

Zobel took Hongwe to their small hut. Because everyone was so busy, they didn't notice that Zobel helped Hongwe.

Hongwe was brave and strong and his body was used to wounds in the forest, but he had to cease himself from what the king's son had done to him. His heart has despair because of the cruel rule of King Herod in the once peaceful and beautiful kingdom ruled by his father.

Even though it was against Zobel's parents to help Hongwe, there was nothing they could do, especially since his behaviour seemed far from other cruel soldiers. Zobel hid her true identity from Hongwe because he might find out that she is a woman and stretch out for Tzungwo. She was afraid but she felt pity for the soldier who suffered the brutality of the king's son.

Hongwe also hid his third eye. He does not remove the bandage from his forehead because his new friend might be afraid of him.

Zobel gave Hongwe her extra clothes that were made by her mother. After a few days, the scars and wounds all over Hongwe's body have healed and he joins as a normal temple construction worker. Because his clothes were ordinary, he was no longer recognized as a former palace soldier who was whipped by Tzungwo. Zobel felt comfortable with Hongwe because of his stability and hard work. She doesn't know but she seems to have strange feelings for Hongwe. She tried to hide her true identity even her voice.

As their companionship lasted, she could no longer explain herself. For the first time, Zobel falls in love. Sometimes she wants to avoid Hongwe but she wants to be with him all the time.

"Are you okay, Zobel? Why do you seem pale? Are you feeling something?" Hongwe patted Zobel's forehead because she might have a fever. Zobel immediately avoided her face because she might show that she is a modest woman and not a man as Hongwe knows her.

As dawn broke, Hongwe invited Zobel to bathe in a clean stream not far from the kingdom before they went to work. The scenery in that place is beautiful and the lapping of the water seems inviting. Zobel didn't want to go but Hongwe grabbed her by the arm and ran away.

"Come on, maybe the soldiers will see us and won't let us bathe," he said as they walked towards the creek.

When they were at the stream, Hongwe immediately took off his upper clothes. His forehead remained tied with a thick cloth so that his third eye could not be seen.

"Come on, Zobel. The water is very cold. Take off your clothes. Let's enjoy the cold water," Hongwe urged Zobel. Zobel's eyes widened upon hearing so she immediately closed her eyes.

She is in awe of Hongwe's seductive and muscular body. She also doesn't want to undress because he might find her secret.

"I don't want to, you are the one to take a bath there," Zobel answered and immediately turned back. She didn't want to keep an eye on Hongwe's naked body visible in the clear water.

Hongwe giggled. "Don't you want to take a bath? What are you hiding in your body? Do you want me to carry you to the water?"

Hongwe joked about making Zobel even more nervous.

"What? I don't want it! How about you, why didn't you take the cloth off you're forehead until you took a bath? What's wrong with that?" she replied nervously.

Because Zobel was turning back, she didn't realize that Hongwe was behind her already.

He immediately carried her up and ran to jump into the clean water. Zobel screamed. Her voice could no longer be hidden because Hongwe could hear her lady's screams. When the water soaked

Zobel's whole body, Hongwe's eyes widened as he saw Zobel's large breasts take shape. He immediately covered his eyes.

Zobel was embarrassed and immediately ran away out of the water. She ran quickly back home to their house. Hongwe was stunned. He didn't think Zobel was a woman.

Chapter 7

Hongwe returned to the forest. He never said goodbye to Zobel. The woman may have been angry with him because of his discovered secret.

He told King Gerom and Queen Ferolina about the erroneous and cruel behavior of King Herod including his son, Prince Tzungwo. Anger appeared on the king's face. He never thought it would happen in the kingdom built by his anancestors.

"That Herod is heartless, savage, and selfish. He is not fit to rule the kingdom my ancestors built. We must take back the kingdom of Tonga!" King Gerom boldly said.

Hongwe spent his life again in the middle of the forest. He practiced throwing spears and karate again.

One day, he saw an old man who seemed to be coiled by a large snake. He cries and asks for help. He immediately helped the old man but the snake was too strong. He couldn't handle its force, especially when the snake transferred to him and tightly coiled around his body. Hongwe seems to be getting weak.

In an instant, he saw in front of him a shiny sword buried in a large rock. He tried to reach it while the big snake continued to coil around his body.

"Hongwe, pull out the sword!" the old man ordered him.

As best as he could he grasped the hilt of the sword and almost forgot how the old man knew his name. The surroundings light up. He too was dazzled by the intense light that came from the sword. Some kind of strength enveloped Hongwe's entire body. The snake was ready to swallow him, so he immediately buried the tip of the sword in its mouth.

Suddenly the big snake disappeared. He searched for its body but it seemed like a smoke had disappeared into thin air. The old man thanked Hongwe.

"You are just like your king's father. It is time for you to lead the kingdom of Tonga again, Hongwe. The king who will defend the realm of the kingdom has risen," said the old man which surprised Hongwe.

Hongwe took the old man to their hut and the king and queen were surprised because they knew the old man. The old man told that he was an emperor of the Moon Kingdom, Emperor Washu. He eyed King Gerom's life and with the power granted to him, Hongwe was born with three eyes. He will be the saviour of the people oppressed by King Herod. Hongwe's third eye came from the dragon, he was the only one who could pull out the magical sword buried in the boulder without the need for magical words.

"Why did you mention Poseude last time?" asked King Gerom to the old man.

"Poseude is a king of snakes. He is a traitor who wants to seize the sword that comes from the power of the dragon. He knows that I know a lot so he wants to kill me. One of those under his power is King Herod and his clan," informed Emperor Washu.

"Can he be defeated?" asked Hongwe.

"Possibly. Only the dragon-marked sword can defeat him."

The King and queen were surprised. King Gerom also notified that the old man appeared before at the palace and Emperor Washu were the same.

King Herod became even more greedy. He is now killing all merchants who fail to pay the right taxes. He also takes the small property of the poor labourers. There is almost nothing left of them. All the young women are sexually abused by Prince Tzungwo.

Zobel is also very scared because she might be discovered as a woman. She still couldn't get Hongwe out of her mind. Only him knew her secret. She doesn't even know where the stranger she first loved is.

Hongwe has said goodbye to his father king and mother queen. This is the right time to fight with King Herod. Emperor Washu, the old man also sent warriors from the Moon Kingdom to help in the fight. Queen Ferolina was restless.

"Take care, my son. You have the blessing of the god of moons, stars, and seas. I still fear for you. I still hope we will see each other again. We love you very much, Hongwe." She hugged Hongwe tightly and couldn't stop tears from falling.

"Do not be scared, my mother queen. I will return, we will claim the kingdom of Tonga again," Hongwe encouraged Queen Ferolina.

Hongwe landed at the palace again and he heard the sickening screams and wails of the people in the village. The merchantmen are being dragged away by the soldiers. Elderly women were also slapped and girls were sexually assaulted face to face. The soldiers laughed as they perform the demonic task.

"Let us enjoy ourselves. We have consent from King Herod and tonight, Prince Tzungwo will be seated as the new king of Tonga. King Tzungwo!" shouted of a soldier with a trumpet for all to hear.

"We must have a young virgin lady offer for him. Anyone who can give to Prince Tzungwo will be given a great reward. No one can escape his will, so get ready because tonight the crown will be successfully transferred to our new king!"

That information of the messenger almost echoed throughout the village. The other women were frightened while crying.

Hongwe remembers Zobel. Maybe, Prince Tzungwo will discover that she is a woman and what will be done to her. He will not allow that to happen.

"Let's get ready, now is the day of the verdict. We will not let the sun go down when the crown will be transferred to the leadership of Tzungwo. He has no right to lead the kingdom of Tonga," Hongwe said to his compatriots. Even, tigers, lions, and big crows are with him in the fight.

The palace was ready for the new regime of Prince Tzungwo. He will inherit the throne. It's only a matter of time before he becomes a full-fledged king. The emperor of Hwaue city and other high leaders of other cities were also there to witness the ceremony. Various designs decorated the entire palace. The poor labourers were offered a lot of food from the yields of their labours. The merchants made huge offerings even though they were penniless. The entire village near the temple was searched to find a virgin woman to offer to the new king because that was his wish after the ceremony.

Everyone was terrified as the kingdom's soldiers ransacked the entire household. By chance, a soldier saw Zobel, she was wearing men's clothes but he noticed the woman's large breasts.

Zobel forgot to wear the binder to her chest so it wouldn't take shape.

"Come on, it looks like you're hiding something! Well, it doesn't look like your true form as a man." A soldier grinned and immediately grabbed Zobel's hand.

"Leave me alone, I am a man and I am a temple worker. Get out of here because this is not the place that you're looking for!" Zobel also shouted.

The soldier grabbed Zobel's chest and touched her soft breast.

"Liar! Impostor, you are a woman and not a man. Prince Tzungwo must not know about this. I guess, you are still a virgin and you are the perfect one to offer to him later. Come, join me and I will surely get a big reward!" The soldier's eyes widened with joy.

"Leave me alone!" Zobel struggled but the soldier was stronger than her.

Zobel's parents also arrived from the plantation and find Zobel fighting a soldier. They were ready to help their daughter but the long weapon was aimed at Zobel.

"Go ahead and try to fight and your daughter's head will be wiped off!"

There was nothing they could do, especially when the soldier punched Zobel in the stomach and completely lost consciousness.

The soldier took Zobel on the horse to the palace. The prince will surely be happy with what he found out. He is eager to get his reward.

"Zobel! Please let her go!"

Zobel's mother almost fainted from crying. For several years, they hid the personality of their daughter so that they would not be like other women that Prince Tzungwo lusted after. Now, there is

22 The Rise Of The Three-Eyed King

nothing they can do because the prince will find out and he will surely abuse her.

Hongwe prepared their weapons for the attack. The sun is about to set and the transfer of crowns to the new king will begin.

The soldiers hid Zobel in a basement. She was guarded by female assistants. Bathed, groomed, and beautified to surprise the new king with their offering. Zobel's crying did not stop. What she feared would happen has come.

She has to get out before the prince does his evil plan for her.

The entire kingdom is also guarded. All the soldiers are also positioned and the deadly weapons are ready in case someone dares to invade the ceremony. The transfer of the crown to Prince Tzungwo was well prepared. King Herod was also very happy because the kingdom will be transferred to his son. No one can take away their power.

The ceremony was about to begin, and the prince's right hand also announced the prepared offering to him. Prince Tzungwo smiled with relief especially when he was informed of the beautiful virgin who would be offered to him after the ceremony.

"That's good news and the best offer into my royalty." He smiled full of lust.

After a while, everyone bowed in homage to the transfer of power from King Herod to Prince Tzungwo.

At the same time as the explosion and loud burst from outside and everyone in the palace was shocked and horrified.

"What is that explosion? Soldiers, check all the surroundings, and don't let that nuisance out of the palace alive!" shouted King Herod's command.

Prince Tzungwo was furious. He doesn't want the ceremony to be revoked.

Tigers, lions, and crows have entered the palace. Despite the arrows flying from the palace tower, that didn't stop them from striking. Soldiers from the Moon kingdom were also flying. The rest of them could not be seen in the air so they could attack the palace. Out of fear, the other emperors in attendance ran out of the palace. They don't want to get into trouble.

Hongwe has also entered the palace. There they met with King Herod.

"Who are you? What stimulated you to destroy my palace? Now you will receive the death penalty! Kill the audacious creature!" bold order of King Herod.

The soldiers immediately rushed but suddenly Hongwe intervened with a sword in his hand. Its blade lit up and almost dazzled the eyes of the soldiers. Even King Herod was surprised. He knew the sword Hongwe was holding.

"Why are you holding the dragon sword? Who are you?" asked the king again as fear took over his entire body.

"I am Hongwe. The only son of the king you usurped the throne from. Today is the day of reckoning. Your wickedness will end!" Hongwe took the cloth covering his forehead so that the king could see the third eye of the dragon.

King Herod's eyes widened even more. He couldn't believe that the most powerful dragon in the forest could live. He will not allow the kingdom to be taken from him again.

The fight lasted more than an hour. The wild animals that accompanied Hongwe from the forest and the invisible soldiers of the moon kingdom helped a lot.

Prince Tzungwo entered Zobel's room that was held. He was amazed by her beauty and could not explain what he felt. For the first time, it seemed that there was something special about Zobel that captured Prince Tzungwo's heart.

But there is no time. The battle continues inside the palace. King Herod also had in his hand the sword with the mark of a great serpent. Their fight with Hongwe continues. King Herod also moved faster. He is also good at karate and moved quickly like a snake. Some soldiers were almost defeated by Hongwe's fellow warriors and the wild beasts from the forest. Hongwe was almost hit in the side by King Herod's sword. Fortunately, he escaped like a dragon.

"You will not win. You are a scourge. No one can beat my power. My ancestry will remain the owners of the kingdom of Tonga!" shouted King Herod.

His eyes were burning. He was very angry with Hongwe.

Unfortunately, the sword reached King Herod's neck. He has fallen into Hongwe's trap.

"That's what you thought. You don't deserve to be king of Tonga or any of your clan. I will take back the kingdom my ancestors bequeathed. This is the end of your evil regime, King Herod!" Hongwe also shouted and was about to cut off the king's head.

"Let him go!" Hongwe turned his head towards the source of the voice.

He was behind him and his heart seemed to be pinched when he saw him holding Zobel, her long hair was loose, she was wearing a thin dress, her body shape was visible and her beauty was reflected. He couldn't understand why his heartbeat suddenly thundered.

"Zobel?" only Hongwe spoke out.

He forgot that King Herod would have been trapped in his hands.

"H-Hongwe? Is that you? Why do you have three eyes? Why did you fight in the kingdom of Tonga? Who you are?" Zobel also asked.

Surprised were also drawn on her beautiful face.

"Do you know each other? And it seems like you two have a reunion," Prince Tzungwo asked insultingly.

"He's the man you chastised a few months ago for not bowing when you came to the temple. He's a soldier of the kingdom," Zobel's only replied. That's what she knew.

King Herod got a chance with his sword, and he threw away the sword that was on his neck. He and Hongwe fought again while Prince Tzungwo held Zobel tightly.

"He is the son of King Gerom. He wants to take back the kingdom of Tonga and I will not allow that. He will die and bring his corpse home to his cowardly king father!" said King Herod accompanied by loud laughter.

Prince Tzungwo was shocked. He did not think that the son of the former king had fooled him.

"You are sorry for entering our territory. Kill him, father king. Cut off his head!" cried Prince Tzungwo boldly.

"I will, my Prince!" King Herod also answered reassuringly.

Even Zobel couldn't believe it. It turns out that her first love was an unidentified prince. She didn't know that the man she helped before was the son of King Gerom. Her heart beats fast.

Power against power. Until King Herod weakened because his snake-marked sword could not withstand the power coming from Hongwe's dragon-marked sword. He fell to the floor and couldn't fight properly. All that was witnessed by Prince Tzungwo.

"In the name of my father, King Gerom, by the power that comes from the gods of the moon, stars, and sea. By the power of the dragon's eye, you will lose your strength and power as a king of Tonga, King Herod!" Hongwe shouted looking up at the sky.

Suddenly the sky brightened, in the darkness of the night. The stars and the moon appeared. Waves from the ocean are surfacing. Thunder rumbled throughout the kingdom. Hongwe plunged his sword into King Herod's forehead with all his might.

"No!" Prince Tzungwo shouted with so much fear.

A loud groan and lamentation also came from King Herod. Thick blood gushed out and in an instant, King Herod turned into a snake. Sluggish and powerless.

Along with King Herod's mutation, Prince Tzungwo also becomes a small serpent. Zobel fainted from so much fear and nervousness that she fell to the floor.

Chapter 8

A month later, the kingdom of Tonga returned to its former magnificence and peace. Everyone was busy. The merchants became energetic and the workers revived because the evil had stopped under the regime of King Herod and Prince Tzungwo.

The new king has been inaugurated. Everyone celebrated. Queen Ferolina burst into tears because she didn't think it would happen again that they would be able to return to the palace. Emperor Washu and King Gerom crowned Hongwe's head.

"Long live the new king. The birth of a new king with three eyes is the saviour of mankind and the kingdom of Tonga!" Emperor Washu declared.

"Long live, King Hongwe! Long live our new king of the Kingdom of Tonga!" shouted all people with so much joy.

They bowed their heads as a sign of respect to the new king.

The sky filled with light again. The stars and the moon are twinkling. Waves kiss in the ocean. The animals in the forest screamed as a sign of their support for the new king.

Other kings and emperors in other kingdoms offered their respective offerings for the new king. The tabernacle was almost filled with gold, silver and diamonds as the beginning of his duty. King Hongwe also thanked them all and promised that he would use them for good and give them to his people in need to make their lives easier.

"My heart rejoices because my dream of having a son to inherit my kingdom has come true. I am in awe of your courage, Hongwe. You deserve to rule the kingdom of Tonga. I know that the kingdom inherited by my ancestors is in good hands again," King Gerom proudly said to Hongwe.

"Let's also thank Emperor Washu because he gave you to us. You are a blessing sent by the god of the stars, the moon, the ocean and even the god of the sun. We are happy with your love for our kingdom, Hongwe," said Queen Ferolina in tears.

"It's an honour my king father and my queen mother. I promise I will protect the kingdom of Tonga and all people as much as I can. I know that the eye of the dragon will be with me in all battles," Hongwe promised and bowed to him the former king and queen as a tribute to his power as a new king.

Emperor Washu's eyes also lit up. At all times he will also be the eyes of King Hongwe and will be his companion in all his battles.

Zobel could not explain her feelings while glancing at the new king. She knew she was no longer worthy of a king's love because she was just an ordinary woman. That did not impede, because King Hongwe opened his love to Zobel.

"I love you, Zobel and you are the only one I want to be with while ruling the kingdom of Tonga. You will be my queen and I will love you with all my heart," King Hongwe said lovingly to Zobel.

Zobel couldn't believe what she heard from the man she loved before.

"But I'm just a lowly woman, I don't come from a royal family and powerful people. I don't deserve you, King Hongwe," she replied painfully.

"That doesn't matter anymore. Do you love me despite my appearance?"

Zobel remained silent and she about to cry.

"Just tell me, Zobel if you can love me even though I have three eyes." King Hongwe's face was sad because maybe Zobel didn't accept him because of his appearance for having three eyes.

Zobel held her face and gave her a simple kiss on the cheek.

"You are the first man I loved and you are also the last man I will love in my whole life, King Hongwe. I had a special feelings for you before. I love you so much even if you still have ten eyes." Joy and love were reflected in Zobel's eyes, as did King Hongwe.

Zobel accepted Hongwe's whole identification at the same time she accepted the sincere love offered to her.

"You make me so much happy, Zobel. I promise to love you and protect you with all my might."

Zobel leaned her head on the wide chest of King Hongwe and felt that her life was safe with the love of the man she loved the most.

King Gerom blessed them. When the full moon arrived, the lavish wedding of King Hongwe and Zobel was held. Emperor Washu and King Gerom's mother, Mother Magda also attended to witness a beautiful and holy ceremony. There was a conflict between Mother Magda and King Gerom and after many years, the wound healed.

Father and son Herod and Tzungwo remained imprisoned in the large dungeon. They only feed on wild animals to survive as serpents. They have no hope of getting out of their dungeon and that is the curse they will carry for the rest of their lives.

"Long live, King Hongwe and his majesty, the new queen of Tonga, Queen Zobel!"

The entire kingdom celebrated the union of King Hongwe and Zobel. Zobel's parents were also very happy because their daughter was in good hands and never expected to be a queen of Tonga.

Their union as the new king and the new queen were peaceful and fruitful.

"I promise to be a good wife and queen to you, my beloved king."

"I will protect you and the whole kingdom my beloved queen."

Their lips kissed with so much love and devotion.

The good rule of the king with three eyes became famous throughout the kingdom and other kingdoms.

The dragon-marked sword encrusted in a precious stone surrounded by a thick crystal with a dragon's eye design flashed. No one can pull it in its permanent place but only King Hongwe.

The kingdom of Tonga and its people live happily ever after.

End

About the Author

Leah Z. Declaro

Leah Z. Declaro is a pure Filipino writer and is currently teaching as a public school teacher. She is residing in Concepcion, Iloilo, Philippines. She is a poet in Hiligaynon, Filipino, and English and has received various certificates and awesome awards in the contests she participated in locally and internationally. She has also had novels published in Dreame with a contract. She is also one of the authors of the book Magkasintahan, Volume XXIV. The author likes to write novels with comedy and drama and this story entitled, The Rise of the Three-eyed King is her first fantasy story.

www.ingramcontent.com/pod-product-compliance
Lightning Source LLC
LaVergne TN
LVHW041601070526
838199LV00046B/2080